10 Minutes till Bedtime

Our Family
One
1-5
6-10
Two
Three and Four
Five
Eight
Seven
Six
Ten
Nine

Snacking

Brushing

Dressing

Reading

Taping

Our Bedtime Tour

Waiting

Fishing

Ant

Goofing

Duck

Boating

FILE EDIT VIEW LABEL SPECIAL
SAVE
FAX
E-MAIL
WWW
HAMSTERS!
Take the
10-MINUTE
BEDTIME TOUR
FREE SNACKS!
CLEAN RESTROOM!
FAMILIES WELCOME!
1 HOPPIN PLACE, NAPVILLE
www.hamstertours.com

10 minutes till Bedtime

PEGGY RATHMANN

SCHOLASTIC INC.
New York Toronto London Auckland Sydney
Mexico City New Delhi Hong Kong

ISBN 0-439-13376-9

12 11 10 9 8 7 6 5 4 3 2 1   0 1 2 3 4 5/0

Printed in the U.S.A.   08

First Scholastic paperback printing, September 2000

Lettering by David Gatti

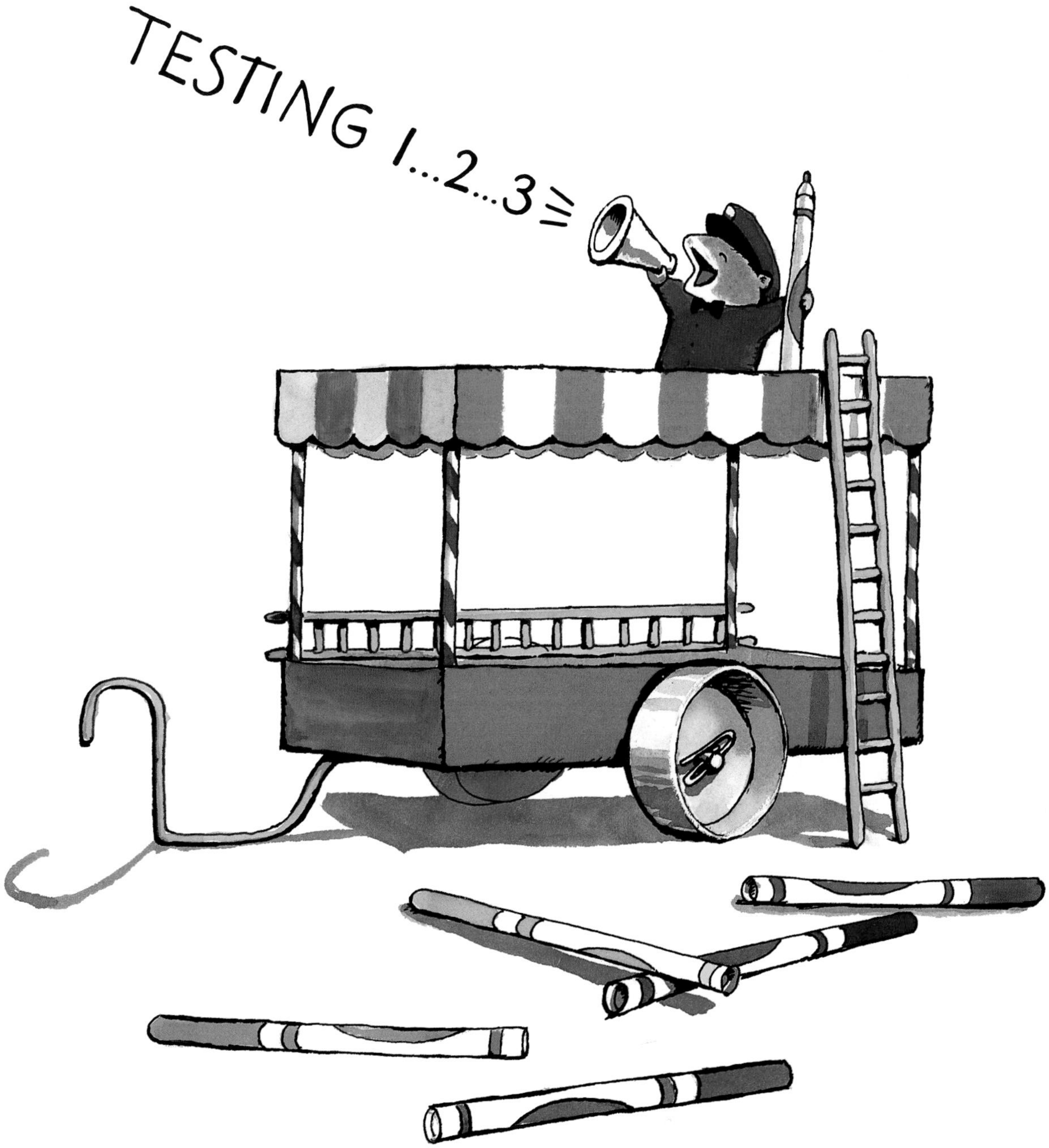
TESTING 1...2...3

10 Minutes till Bedtime
FAMILY LIFE
DO YOU KNOW WHAT YOUR CHILDREN ARE DOING? Experts at universities study average bedtime routines
TRAVEL
TOURS RESORTS ADVENTURES
STAY IN A REAL TREEHOUSE
SPEND A WEEK IN THE WOODS
Eat like a bird! Sing songs! Have fun!
55-613-21
WEATHER BALLOONS
CHEAP TRANSPORTATION whichever way the wind blows
Visit NEW ZEALAND
WORK ON A FARM JUST LIKE BABE!
Why spend another vacation doing the same old thing? Come get really dirty chasing sheep around! Talk to ducks!
$957.00 U.S.
SARGASSO SEA SAILING ADVENTURES
$749.00
FLOAT MOTIONLESS FOR DAYS, MONTHS, EVEN YEARS IN A BIG PATCH OF SEAWEED. TOUR LEAVES FROM HERE PROMPTLY AND RETURNS LATER. IF YOU NEED TO KNOW MORE, TOUR IS NOT FOR YOU. TOTAL COST FAR EXCEEDS ANY PRICE QUOTED
SWIM
Join a group of ocean lovers on a 3-year expedition tracking WHALES!
IMPROVE YOUR STROKE!
FIRST INTERNATIONAL HOPSCOTCH FESTIVAL
SATURDAY MORNING
RUBY'S DRIVEWAY
BRING CHALK.
HAMSTERS!
Take the 10-MINUTE BEDTIME TOUR
FREE SNACKS! CLEAN RESTROOM!
FAMILIES WELCOME!
1 HOPPIN PLACE, NAPVILLE
www.hamstertours.com
FREE AD!
DONT MISS THIS SPECIAL INTRODUCTORY OFFER. OUR TRAVEL SECTION WILL RUN YOUR LOCAL AD AT NO CHARGE! ACT NOW! TO PLACE YOUR AD CALL (415) 440-1358
WANTED: Housesitter to feed the GORILLA for 2 weeks during my vacation. Please call Joe at the Zoo.
VISIT A REAL CASTLE AND STAY IN THE DUNGEON!
MAIL YOURSELF TO EXOTIC DESTINATIONS
FOR DETAILS, WRITE TO: FLAT STANLEY TOURS
SWEET RETREATS
LEARN CAKE DECORATING WHILE VACATIONING IN LOVELY NAPVILLE
SESSION I: BUTTERCREAM STARS AND GARLANDS
SESSION II: SUGAR FLOWERS AND FIGURINES
FOR RESERVATIONS CALL 555-4821

THEY'RE COMING!!

1 HOPPIN PLACE
hi

ALL ABOARD

9
Minutes
till
Bedtime

Wheeeee
NINE MINUTES

8 Minutes till Bedtime
EIGHT MINUTES

COOKIES
eat

7
Minutes
till
Bedtime

SEVEN MINUTES
toof

6
Minutes
till
Bedtime

SIX MINUTES
hee hee

5 Minutes till Bedtime
FIVE MINUTES

read
10 Minutes till Bedtime

MORE COMING

more!

WELCOME

1 HOPPIN PLACE

4 Minutes till Bedtime

balloon
FOUR MINUTES

3 Minutes till Bedtime
bye-bye

HEY, WAIT!

2 Minutes till Bedtime
TWO MINUTES

potty

1 Minute till Bedtime

duck
ONE MINUTE

Bedtime!

uh-oh

faster

STOP!
sleepy

BED

TIME!
BED TIME!

GOOD NIGHT, HAMSTERS!
The 10-MINUTE BEDTIME TOUR
IS CLOSED
SWEET DREAMS!